CHOWDER

THE BRUISED BLUENANA

THE MEACH HARVEST

EGMONT
We bring stories to life

First published in Great Britain 2010
by Egmont UK Limited
239 Kensington High Street, London W8 6SA

Cartoon Network, the logo, Chowder and all
related characters and elements are trademarks of and
© 2010 Cartoon Network.

Adapted by Brenda Apsley
Based on original storylines by C. H. Greenblatt,
Danielle McCole, Peter Browngardt and William Reiss

ISBN 978 1 4052 5542 4

1 3 5 7 9 10 8 6 4 2

Printed and bound in Great Britain by the CPI Group

FSC
Mixed Sources
Product group from well-managed
forests and other controlled sources

Cert no. TT-COC-002332
www.fsc.org
© 1996 Forest Stewardship Council

Egmont is passionate about helping to preserve the world's remaining ancient forests.
We only use paper from legal and sustainable forest sources.

This book is made from paper certified by the Forestry Stewardship Council (FSC),
an organisation dedicated to promoting responsible management of forest resources.
For more information on the FSC, please visit www.fsc.org. To learn more about
Egmont's sustainable paper policy, please visit www.egmont.co.uk/ethical

THE BRUISED BLUENANA

Chapter One

One afternoon, Chowder was at the Marzipan City Farmers' Market. Was he buying bluenanas? Grabbing green grapples?

No, he was wiggling his finger around in his belly button – and he was being watched.

Chowder pulled out a big piece of belly button fluff, which he tasted, salted – and *ate*.

Up on the roof of Gazpacho's food stall, Panini had her binoculars trained on him. "Smart … manly …" she murmured. "Mmm … sophisticated."

Panini had a crush on Chowder. A *major* crush. A crush that he didn't return. But that was nothing to a girl blinded by love.

"Chowder – what more could a girl want?" she

said, putting on her best kiss-me-now-and-make-it-good lipstick. "Time to catch me my man!"

With belly-button-fluff being a rather light snack, Chowder was still hungry. He followed his nose to his friend Gazpacho's stall. "Hey, Gazpacho, I got a need to feed," he said. "What's looking good today?"

Gazpacho pulled off his hat to reveal a scary sight. "Besides my new hairstyle?" he said.

But Chowder only had eyes for the food. "Let's see," he said. "I'm in the mood for some, um ..."

"Fish?" Gazpacho suggested, as a large hook swung out of nowhere and snagged Chowder, reeling him upwards.

"No, something more like …" said Chowder. Then he noticed that his feet were no longer on the ground. "Ow! Hey! Yikes!"

Helpless, like a fish on a line, Chowder was pulled up onto the roof where he saw an all-too-familiar smiley pink face and a pair of large ears.

"Hi, Chowder," cooed Panini, still dangling him from her fishing rod.

"I'm not your boyfriend!" he yelled automatically as he tried to make his escape.

But Panini wasn't about to lose her prize catch, and as Chowder leapt away she reeled him back one, two, three, four times.

"I love you, num-nums," whispered Panini, puckering up for a kiss. "I really do."

That did it. "Arrrgh!" screamed Chowder. "Gazpacho, help! I'm being held by a madwoman."

"Oh, my gosh! A madwoman?" gasped Gazpacho who, faced with rescuing his friend or hiding, jumped into a barrel of pickles.

Chowder was on his own. "What do you want from me, Panini?" he demanded.

Panini smiled a smile that made Chowder shiver. "I just wanna ... *look* at you."

Yikes! Chowder had to get away. Soon. Very soon. As soon as possible. Now. Right now. Yesterday, even. Any way he could.

He lunged forwards, his mouth open wide, and – **snap, chomp, chew!** – bit into the fishing rod, gnawing it in two. Freed, Chowder fell down from the roof and landed in front of Gazpacho's stall. But his friend was still hiding in the pickle

barrel, and standing in his place behind the counter was … Panini!

"How's about a piece of my heart?" She grabbed Chowder and pulled him over to her side of the counter. "Come here ..."

"Arrrrrrgh! No! Get off me!" screamed Chowder as he slammed into a crate of bluenanas – **CRASH!** – stomping and trampling on them as he tried to run away.

It was always going to take a lot to get Gazpacho out of his pickle-barrel hiding place, but the harm being done to the bluenanas did the trick.

"Stop!" he cried. *"You're bruising the bluenanas!"*

Chowder picked up a particularly pummelled bluenana. "Oh, my gosh," he cried, gazing at it. "I'm so sorry, bluenanas. You know I'd never do anything to hurt you, my poor sweet blue babies."

"Did you say *babies*?" said Panini. An idea so weird, so crazy, so *Panini* was growing in her furry pink head. It had to work! "Chowder, what did you do to *our baby*?"

"Our baby?" asked Chowder, confused. What was Panini talking about?

"Yes," said Panini quickly, snatching the badly bruised bluenana from Chowder. "We have to nurse it back to health."

"We?" repeated Chowder.

"What?" asked Panini.

"You said we."

"Said we what?"

"Who said what?" Gazpacho cut in.

"She said we," Chowder explained.

"You?" said Gazpacho, puzzled. "Me?"

"No, me," said Chowder.

"We?" questioned Panini.

"Who?" asked Gazpacho.

Chowder stopped. "I don't even know any more!"

"Chowder, our baby is sick," said Panini firmly. Her plan had worked! Her cutie-patootie was so confused that he'd say yes to anything. "As parents, we have to help it heal ..."

Her next word made Chowder shudder with fear: "... TOGETHER!"

Chapter Two

Chowder gulped. *Huh? Did he hear that right?*
"We?" he asked again weakly.

Panini moved closer. "Yes," she whispered.
"Our love will heal this baby."

"But there is no love between us," he pointed
out plainly.

"Don't say that in front of the baby," scolded
Panini.

"The baby can't hear," said Chowder. "It
doesn't have ears."

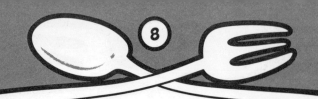

For Panini, this was easily solved. She took out a pen and drew an ear on the bluenana. "Now it does."

Chowder gasped. The bluenana could hear? Now he'd have to watch what he said …

Panini grabbed hold of Chowder and dragged him away. "Now hurry, future husband," she said. "There's no time to lose. Quick!"

It became clear to Chowder that Panini wasn't going to take no for an answer. "Uh, how long's it going to take to heal the baby?" he asked.

"Hopefully … weeks," Panini replied.

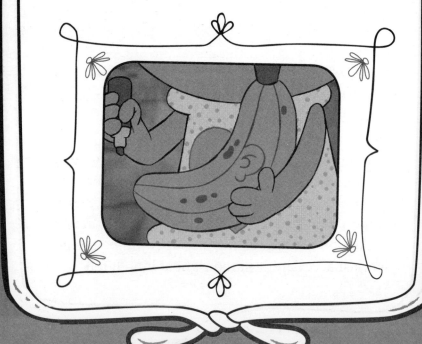

Chowder's heart sank. *"Weeks?"* he repeated, a look of dread on his face. Weeks with Panini? All alone? With no escape? It was a fate worse than dieting.

But what could he do? There was nothing he cared about more than food, like the bluenana baby. "Bye, Gazpacho," he said sadly. "Guess I'll see you in a few weeks."

"No worries, buddy," said Gazpacho, jumping back into his safe, madwoman-free pickle barrel. "I'll be right here."

In a flash, Panini fashioned a horrible baby sling so Chowder could carry the bluenana everywhere he went. Then she insisted on escorting him to his apprenticeship at Mung Daal's Catering Company.

"Oh, Chowder, you make such a handsome baby-daddy," she said, as he cringed. "Have a super day at work, Number One Dad."

Panini was looking more and more crazy-eyed, so Chowder ran inside and quickly slammed the door shut: **THONK!** But there was Panini, right behind him like a piece of furry, pink cling film ...

As Chowder sat eating his super-jumbo before-work snack, Panini stared right at him. It felt weird. Worrying. He almost couldn't taste just how super-jumbo-yummy his snack was.

Chowder had to get rid of Panini. Maybe she could take a hint. "Bye," he said.

But Panini just carried on staring.

"Bye," Chowder repeated, a little louder this time.

Panini stared.

Chowder began to panic. He had to do something.

"Brring, brring, brring, brring, brring," he said in his best I'm-a-phone voice, picking up the bluenana baby like it was a mobile and holding it to his ear.

"Hello?" he said. "Mm-hmm. OK, I'll tell her. Panini, Ms Endive says she needs you in her kitchen."

The pretend message from her boss did the trick. "Oh, OK," said Panini. "Well, see you later."

Panini started to walk away, but she was back in a micro-second. "Oh, wait," she said. "I forgot to tell you, don't worry because I'll be right back. So if you need me for anything, remember, I'll be *right back*."

Chowder ignored her and Panini started to

walk away again, but was back even faster this time. "Right back!" she said. "Do you need me yet? I mean, for the baby?"

Chowder had heard enough. He picked up a megaphone and bellowed into it. "BYE!"

"OK," said Panini, getting the message at last. "Bye."

When Panini had gone, Chowder started to relax a little, until – **brring, brring!** – the bluenana phone really did ring!

Chowder had a good idea who was calling.

"Hello?" he said. "No, Panini, we're fine. OK." Chowder hung up the bluenana phone.

It was clear that he wasn't going to shake off Panini on his own. He needed advice. But who could he go to with his troubles?

Chapter Three

"Mung, what am I gonna do?" Chowder asked his boss desperately. Being married to a bad-tempered mushroom fairy for 450 years made Mung Daal a good source of advice. "Panini's gonna keep on coming round here as long as our pretend baby has a bruise on it."

As soon as he said it, the thought of repeat visits from Panini made his arms start to panic and flap around uncontrollably!

Shnitzel, Mung's rock-monster helper, grabbed Chowder and held him in a soothing rock-monster-hold until his arms calmed down.

"Thanks, Shnitzel," said Chowder.

"Radda-radda," said Shnitzel. No problem!

"Well, you know what you've got to do, Chowder," Mung finally replied.

Disappear? thought Chowder. So he did just that.

"No, Panini will still find you. Women can smell fear," Mung advised to the empty space where Chowder had been.

Chowder reappeared. So, if disappearing wasn't going to work, what was?

"What you've got to do is heal that bluenana as fast as you can," Mung told his apprentice.

"Right," said Chowder. "Heal the bluenana. I get it. Now what makes you feel better when you're sick? Hey, I know – hot soup! Hot soup always does the trick."

Moments later, Chowder was standing over a pot of super-hot soup that sizzled and bubbled. **Shlop-shloop! Shlop-shloop!**

Did he blow on the soup to cool it down before feeding it to the bluenana baby? Did he offer the baby a tiny taste on an itty-bitty little baby-sized spoon?

Splosh! Chowder hurled the baby into the red-hot liquid, and it bubbled and sizzled, just like the soup.

"Oh, no!" Chowder gasped, gazing at the burned bluenana, which was now covered in blisters as well as bruises.

OK, so soup wasn't going to make the baby better, but Chowder came up with another get-well-quick idea. "Massage!" he said. "I'll massage the bluenana back to health."

Did he lay soft, healing hands on the baby bluenana? Did he gently soothe its blisters and bruises away?

Smash! Chowder picked up a giant wooden mallet and banged it down on the poor bluenana, over and over again. **Smash! Whack! Thwack!**

After hundreds of hits, Chowder checked on the bluenana to see how it was doing. *Oh, no!* It didn't look any better at all. In fact, it looked a lot worse, and now had bumps to go along with the blisters and bruises!

"Maybe I didn't do it enough times," Chowder said, and he started whacking the bluenana again, even harder this time. **SMASH! WHACK! THWACK!**

When his arm got tired, he stopped banging

and decided to try something else. But what?

Of course! "Bed's the place to be if you're not well," said Chowder. What the baby needed was quiet bed rest. So he took it home, laid it in a cradle, and rocked it gently as he sang:

> **Lullaby and good night**
> **My pretend banana baby**
> **Please get better very quickly**
> **So Panini will stop bothering me**
> **All the time**
> **La-la-la-laaaa ...**

The lullaby didn't help the baby, but it did a lot for Chowder. He found his song so soothing that his eyelids began to feel heavy. He slumped forwards and fell asleep, snoring. **Zzzzzzz ...**

Which is how Panini found him.

Chapter Four

"Hello, Chowder," Panini chirped.

The sound of her voice was enough to jerk Chowder wide awake. "Aah!"

Panini gave Chowder one of her extra-long, lingering love-looks, and noticed that his face was covered in mush. It was as if he'd suddenly grown a beard. A blue beard.

Panini liked his new look, but then again, she liked everything about Chowder. "Digging the new beard," she said.

Beard? What beard? **Slurp-slurp!** Chowder licked his mushy chin. "Huh? Bluenana mush?" he realised in a quiet panic. *Baby* bluenana mush!

Chowder turned his back on Panini and tried to wipe the bluenana-baby-mush-beard off his face before she could see.

When he looked down into the cradle, he gasped. The baby bluenana was hurt. Mushed. Smushed. Mashed. Mangled.

Panini still hadn't seen the damage. "What did you say, Daddy num-nums?" she asked.

"W-what?" gabbled Chowder in a fright. He blocked her view of the cradle. "Nothing."

"How's our baby?" asked Panini.

"Fine," said Chowder.

"Did it miss me?"

"Nope."

"So is it feeling better?"

"Yep," said Chowder. "All better." He had to get rid of her – and fast. "Go home."

"But I want to see it," said Panini.

"No, it said no visitors," said Chowder.

But Panini knew something was wrong. "Chowder, let me see our baby!" she yelled, pushing past him and gazing into the cradle.

When Panini saw bluenana baby mush, her eyes opened wide in horror. *"What did you do to our baby?"* she screamed.

What could Chowder say? Not a lot. "I didn't mean to ..." he said weakly.

Panini was not happy. At all. But maybe this could make her plan even better ... "It's obvious that you are a bad parent and you're not fit to take care of this baby unsupervised," she told him sternly. "Come here."

Chowder moved towards Panini. Slowly. Very slowly. What was she going to do?

He found out a moment later, when Panini took a leap and landed extremely close to him. As close to him as possible. So close that she was *inside his clothes.*

Her pink head popped out from his shirt, right next to his. "For the sake of our baby, I must never, ever leave your side until it's healed," smiled Panini, her face just a millimetre away from his. "Understand?"

Chowder understood all right.

Panini would be with him for every hour, every minute, every second of every day until

the bluenana baby got better. She would be right there with him always. Forever and ever. Until the end of time.

Chowder tried to speak, but as Panini looked at him, crazy-eyed and determined, no sound came from his lips.

But one big tear rolled down his doomed, defeated face ...

Later, Panini and Chowder took their bluenana baby to the park.

"Did you ever notice the baby has your eyes? Oh, they're beautiful, just like you," said Panini, reaching out to Chowder. "Touch."

"Arrgh!" Chowder screamed.

"Boo hoo," boo-hooed the baby.

"Chowder, stop," said Panini. "You're making the baby cry. You'd better make it happy or else it won't heal."

Chowder stopped and remembered his plan. He needed the bluenana baby to get better to be rid of Panini.

Back at home, Chowder gave the baby a bath. "Is it healed now?" he asked.

"No, it needs to be fed," said Panini.

So – **splat! splot!** – Chowder drenched the bluenana in baby milk.

"How about now?" asked Chowder. "Healed?"

"Almost," said Panini. "Kiss the baby."

"You promise that'll heal it?"

"I promise. Now close your eyes."

"What for?" asked Chowder.

"To heal the baby!" insisted Panini.

"Right," said Chowder, closing his eyes and making kissy-kissy noises. **Smick-smack!**

Panini moved closer. "You're the best, Daddy bear," she whispered.

Something told Chowder that something was very, very, very, very wrong. He opened his eyes.

Panini's lips were almost touching his!

"Argggh!" he cried. *"Noooooo!"*

Panini had almost kissed him! He had to get away from her, *now*. But where could he hide?

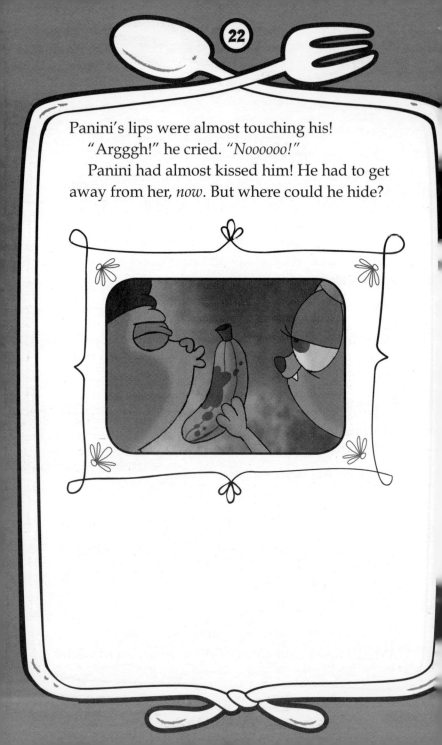

Chapter Five

Chowder ripped off the shirt he had been forced to share with Panini and ran bare-bellied all the way to the Farmers' Market. There he saw the perfect hiding place.

He took a flying leap right into Gazpacho's pickle barrel.

"Uh, Chowder? It's a little tight in here," said Gazpacho, who was wedged in beside him.

A moment later, they were both squeezed out of the pickle barrel – **pop! pop!** – like corks from a bottle.

"Oof," said Gazpacho. "So, uh, are you going to tell me what happened to your shirt?"

Chowder covered his bits and started telling the story from the very beginning. "Well, it all started when I was walking through the Farmers' Market," he explained. "I picked some fluff out of my belly button and tasted it, but I thought it needed some salt, so I salted it. And then it tasted really good."

"Fast forward," suggested Gazpacho.

"And then I said, 'We?' and Panini said, 'What?' and I said, 'You said we' and Panini said,

'Said we what?' and you said, 'Who said what?' and I said ..."

"Keep going," said Gazpacho.

"And then you said, 'So, uh, are you going to tell me what happened to your shirt?' and I covered myself ..." said Chowder.

"Ah, I get it now," Gazpacho nodded. "Mother says that when a woman pretends she has a fruit baby with you and jumps into your clothes, there's only one thing to do."

Gazpacho began to disappear.

"No, women can smell fear," Chowder told

his fading friend, remembering Mung's words.

Gazpacho reappeared. "Aw, nuts ..."

A sobbing Panini arrived with the bluenana baby, having sneakily put drops in her eyes to make herself cry. "Chowder, Chowder, Chowder, come home," she wailed loudly. "Boo-hoo! The baby misses you. *I* miss you. I miss you so much it hurts!"

Chowder ignored her. He had come up with a new plan to solve the Panini problem and he was sure this one would work.

"Hey, Panini, guess what?" he smiled.

"You love me?" said Panini hopefully.

"Ew," said Chowder. "No, we're off the hook. I found the baby bluenana's real mother."

Enter Gazpacho, dressed as Mrs Bluenana.

"Oh, my baby," he wailed in his best bluenana-mummy voice. "Thanks for taking care of him."

But the disguise didn't fool Panini at all. "It's an *it*, not a he!" she snapped. "If you were really its mother, you'd know that."

"Gimme that baby. Ooo, gimme that baby!" moaned Gazpacho.

Panini was so mad that her arms and legs went out of control! It wasn't until Shnitzel arrived and

put her in a rock-monster hold that she calmed
down a little.

"Thanks, Shnitzel," said Panini.

"Radda-radda," said the rock monster. *No
problem.*

But Panini was still angry with Gazpacho.
"Ain't nothing coming between me and my
baby," she hissed, starting her sharp cat-claws
whirring like mean chainsaws. **Sssz z z z z z z!**

"Arrrgh!" screamed Gazpacho. "Chowder!"

Seeing his friend in such deep trouble made
Chowder feel frightened, so he drew a little
mouth around his belly button.

"I'm scared, Chowder," said the tiny tummy-mouth.

"I'm scared, too, Mr Tummy," Chowder answered. At least he wasn't alone!

"Take that! And that!" shouted Panini, smacking Gazpacho with the bluenana baby, which suddenly split open – **SMACK! S-s-s-quelch!**

Uh-oh, thought Chowder. *What that poor bluenana baby needs is for its real mummy to arrive right now.*

Ta-da! That's just what happened next! The bluenana mother suddenly arrived. The *real*

bluenana mother this time. Not a market-stall-man dressed up in a giant bluenana skin and a dress. No, this was the baby bluenana's real mother bluenana.

"Hey," said Panini, looking her over. "It's not a pretend mum. It's a real mum."

"The real mum?" repeated Chowder.

"The real mum?" re-repeated Gazpacho, and jumped back into his pickle barrel.

"Look what you've done! You should be ashamed of yourselves," yelled the bluenana mother. She grabbed the little heap of peel and mush that was her baby and hurried away.

Chowder felt bad for taking such terrible care of her baby. "Um, OK," he said. "Well, bye."

Panini felt bad, too, and she began to cry. "Boo-hoo! Boo-hooooo!" she blubbed. This time, her tears were real.

Chowder felt sorry for Panini. Before he could stop himself, he gave her a quick hug. Then he realised what he was doing and made a fast exit before she could hug him back.

"I knew it, you do love me," sang Panini.

"I'm not your boyfriend!" called Chowder as he sped away.

"Music to my ears," sighed Panini happily.

"I'M NOT YOUR BOYFRIEND!" Chowder yelled again. Then he had the Ultimate Mega No-More-Panini Wonder-Plan. Maybe, just maybe, if he told her he wasn't her boyfriend one hundred-billion-kajillion-shmapillion times, she would *finally* get it.

It was worth a try, right?

THE END

THE BRUISED BLUENANA GALLERY

Chowder's belly button fluff needs some salt.

Panini reels Chowder in for a kiss.

Chowder tries
to run away.

The bruised
bluenana baby.

Chowder babysits ... badly.

Panini gets very close to Chowder.

Gazpacho –
Master of Disguise.

The baby's real
mother shows up.

THE MEACH HARVEST GALLERY

Chowder's all-time hero.

Someone's ordered mince meach pie.

Mung's meach memories.

Disguised as Girl Guides ...

... and as a mariachi band.

Chowder asks nicely.

Chowder gets his hero's autograph.

The pie customer gets his just desserts.

THE MEACH HARVEST

Chapter One

Chowder came into the huge kitchen of Mung Daal's Catering Company and called out to Shnitzel, his rock-monster colleague.

"Shnitzel!" yelled Chowder, holding up a poster of their boss. It showed Mung as a young man, posing proudly with cooking spoon and fork like a superhero chef. Which he was ... to Chowder, at least. "Look at this kicking poster Mung gave me. Isn't it the best thing you've seen in your entire life?"

"Radda. Radda-radda," said Shnitzel. He seemed to agree, but there was no way of telling.

"Yeah, I know," Chowder went on. "Mung's the best. He can do anything."

Mung overheard his words, and tried his best to look modest. "Oh, that's not true, Chowder," he said. "You know I can't raise the dead."

But Chowder knew better. "You just haven't tried hard enough."

Truffles the mushroom-fairy flew in. She didn't share Chowder's admiration for her husband, Mung. "Aw, enough with the love-fest already," she nagged, waving an order form. "We got an order for mince meach pie."

At those words, Mung turned a very pale shade of pale, one eye went all red and screwy, and a look of sheer horror appeared on his face.

"M-m-mince meach?" he stammered, starting to panic. "*M-m-mince* m-m-meach? Arrrgh! N-n-n-n-n-noooooo!"

Mung's screams and cries of terror filled not only the kitchen, but every corner of Marzipan City. He was so frightened that he had to hide somewhere. Anywhere.

Did he flee behind the fridge? Cower in the curtains? No, he jumped into the compost bin. Chowder, Shnitzel and Truffles watched in astonishment.

"Uh, Mung …" Chowder said slowly. "Why are you hiding in the potato peelings?"

"I'm n-not h-hiding," Mung said. "I'm j-just w-waiting until the c-customer g-goes away." He paused. "Forever."

What was all the fuss about? wondered Chowder. What could be so scary about making something as easy as – well, *pie*?

"Aren't we gonna make the mince meach pie?" he asked his boss.

"M-m-m-mince m-m-m-meach?" babbled Mung. The words seemed to strike terror into his heart, and fear filled his eyes. It was as if he was remembering something scarier than the scariest scare that had ever scared.

Chowder tried a little flattery. "Mung, you *have* to make this dish. You're my hero."

Blocking out Chowder's words, Mung hum-de-hummed and la-de-daaed. "I can't hear yoooou!" he sang-de-sang.

"Give it up, kid," Truffles advised Chowder. She had seen Mung in this sort of mood before. "When he sits in the potato peelings, there's no talking to him."

"Mung?" Chowder pleaded. He didn't want to give up. But when he looked from the cool, confident poster-Mung to the real Mung, who was shivering and shaking, blubbing and babbling, Chowder sighed a big sigh. Then an even bigger sigh – and tore the poster in half.

Chowder's all-time hero had become a total *zero*.

He pushed Mung's compost bin into the room where the pie customer was waiting.

"I'm sorry, Mister," Chowder told him sadly. "Mung can't make your pie." He stopped, not believing what he was about to say. "He's too scared to be a chef any more."

Flies buzzed around as the lid of the rubbish bin opened, and Mung's head appeared in a shower of leftovers and potato peelings.

"Has the customer gone?" whispered Mung, still panicked. But when he spotted the customer,

he cringed and ducked back into the bin.

"See?" said Chowder. "What did I tell you?"

The customer looked at Mung in disgust. "I thought this was a catering company," he growled as he headed for the door. "Not a nursery for scared little poopy *crybabies*."

That final insult did the trick! "No one calls Mung Daal a scared little poopy crybaby!" he shouted from the safety of the bin.

"Pack the gear," Mung told Chowder bravely. "We're going on a meach hunt!"

"Yes!" said Chowder. His hero was back!

Chapter Two

Later that day, Chowder was singing happily as Shnitzel's rock-monstrously ugly snail-car sped out of Marzipan City.

I'm gonna eat some meaches
I'll eat them on the beaches
They taste like ...
Like ...

Chowder stopped and looked back at Mung. "Uh, what do meaches taste like?" he asked.

Mung looked rather poorly. He was a very sickly shade of lime green, and he trembled and shook as beads of sweat trickled down his face.

"Mung, you don't look so good," said Chowder. "Are you gonna barf?"

"Radda?" said Shnitzel, which was Shnitzel-speak for 'If you're gonna hurl, please don't do it in my car'.

"I am not going to –" Mung took a deep, deep breath, "– urgh ... barf."

Chowder kept on. "You look like you're going to barf."

"Well – urgh – I'm not gonna," Mung insisted, turning even lime-greener.

"This is what you look like," Chowder told Mung, pulling his very best I'm-feeling-like-a-hunk-of-rotten-aubergine-at-the-bottom-of-a-rubbish-skip face.

"Urgh ... stop it, Chowder," Mung pleaded weakly.

"OK, OK," said Chowder, taking no notice at all. "You know what makes *me* barf? Sour milk. Aw, I drank a whole glass once on a hot day like today. Just thinking about the smell ..."

That did it! **YERTCH! Yertch yerrtch yeeerrrrrtch.**
Bits of Mung's breakfast spattered and spotted
the whole of the inside of Shnitzel's car.

Told you so! said the look on Chowder's face.
"I *knew* you were going to barf!" he told Mung
happily.

"Radda-radda-radda," grumbled Shnitzel,
screeching the car to a halt. "Radda-radda!"
Which was Shnitzel-speak for – well, it's not very
polite, so we'll just skip that part.

As Shnitzel hosed the car clean, Chowder got
straight to the point. "Why do meaches freak you
out?" he asked Mung.

"I can't talk about it," Mung replied shakily.
"It's so painful."

"I understand," said Chowder, even though
he didn't. Now he really, *really* wanted to know
about meaches.

When they got going again, Chowder decided
to have another try at cracking the mysterious
meachy mystery.

"Can you talk about it now?" he asked Mung.
"No, Chowder."
"How about now?" Chowder persisted.
"Not now."

"Now?"

"Way too painful."

"I bet you can talk about it now."

"Not yet!"

Shnitzel decided to join in. "Radda-radda?" he asked.

"No means no, Shnitzel," said Mung.

"How about now?" tried Chowder. He just had to know!

Seeing that Chowder wasn't going to give up, Mung finally agreed to spill the beans. "Well, OK," he began. "It was fifty years ago today ..."

Chapter Three

"Never mind, we're here!" Chowder shouted. They were passing a road sign that said:

WELCOME TO MEACH FIELDS

"B-but ..." said Mung.

Chowder ignored him. "We're here, we're here, we're here!" he cried excitedly.

Mung started to panic again. "U-uuur! Stop!" he cried. "This is close enough."

Shnitzel stopped the car and Chowder jumped out. Mung didn't. He was too busy cowering and shaking in the back seat.

"Hey, Mung!" Chowder yelled into his boss's gigantic ear.

"Arrgh!" Mung screamed in alarm. "Ooo," he panted. "Ooo, er, hello, Chowder."

Mung's terror captured Chowder's attention again. "Why are you so scared of the meaches?" he asked. "Do they taste really gross?"

"No, not at all," said Mung. "Mince meach pie is the most delicious pie in the whole world."

"The whole world ... ?" echoed Chowder.

"According to pie scientists," Mung was saying, but Chowder wasn't listening. To a boy

who loved food as much as Chowder, this was like winning the lottery, finding pirate's treasure and being given a lifetime supply of earwax remover all at the same time!

He tried to imagine how the meach pie would taste, and then he started to drool. And the more he imagined, the more he drooled. The more he drooled, the more he imagined. "I wanna make mince meach pie ..." he murmured in a daze, dreaming of seventh helpings.

"Ha!" cackled Mung madly. "That's what I said once. It was fifty years ago today. I was young.

Arrogant. Handsome. So very handsome ..."

Mung's thoughts took him back in time, and he began to tell his terrible tale. "You see, the queen meach is a peaceful and flavourful fruit," he said, "but her servants are vicious and bitter. They don't give up easily ..."

When young Mung had first seen the queen meach, she was sitting at the top of the magnificent meach tree. He had taken her in his arms and she had seemed quite happy about it. "Tee-hee! Oh, a man," she giggled.

But the queen's fierce meach guards were not very happy about her kidnapping. **"Grrrr-aaa!"** they snarled as they chased after him.

Somehow, Mung escaped with the queen.

"Now it's just me and meach," he smiled, and soon the pie was made.

"My first mince meach pie," Mung told Chowder, remembering that long-ago day. "It was everything I thought it would be."

But that very night, when young Mung was taking a shower, his happy hum-de-dums turned to screams of terror – "Arrgh! Oooo!" – as the meach guards appeared from nowhere and attacked him!

And that wasn't the end. Next morning, as young Mung made his breakfast, more meach guards flew out at him – "Arrgh! Oooo! Owww!" he screamed.

Day and night, night and day, the siege went on – "Arrgh! Oooo! Owww! Urrgh!" The days turned into weeks, and weeks turned into months. The seasons came and went, and still the siege went on. "Arrgh! Oooo! Owww! Urrgh! HEELLLP!"

Mung was still lost in his memories. "The meaches attacked again and again and again and

again and again and again and again and again andagainandagainandagain," he said, reliving the terror. "Every day for … twenty-five years."

He paused. "Meaches hold one heck of a grudge."

The meach guards finally left Marzipan City, but it took Mung and the other citizens many years to recover.

"They broke my spirit," he confessed. "And all my bones. They even ate my hair. And that's why I don't ever want to make that dish again. Ever again. Ever, ever, ever again."

"I understand now," said Chowder. "Mung,

I think it's really brave of you to face your fears like this."

"I'm not facing my fears," said Mung quickly, then he was quiet for what seemed to Chowder like a very long time before adding, "*You* are."

Yikes! thought Chowder. "What?"

"I'm not going anywhere near those blood-thirsty things," Mung announced. "You and Shnitzel do it."

The conversation was not going the way Chowder wanted. He didn't like the sound of those meach guards, and he started to panic at the thought of twenty-five years of hurt. Chowder was an eater, not a fighter.

"You have to help us, Mung," he said. "You're the world's greatest chef."

Chowder had repaired Mung's poster with sticky tape, and he held it up to show his boss. "I even fixed your poster," he said.

But Mung wasn't budging from the car. "If you come back alive, I'll autograph it," he said.

Chowder ripped up the poster again in pure frustration. "C'mon, Shnitzel," he sighed. "We have to show Mung that a *good* chef can conquer *any* food."

But Shnitzel was having none of that, and started to walk away. "Radda-radda," he said, Shnitzel-speak for 'I'm outta here'.

"Get back here, Shnitzel!" ordered Mung.

"Grrrrr?" growled Shnitzel, but he did as he was told.

"Yes!" yelled Chowder as he faced the meach fields. There, in the distance, was the meach tree where they would find the queen.

And stationed in a ring around the tree, like a Dastardly Doughnut of Doom, were countless numbers of fierce meach guards.

What had Chowder got himself into?

Chapter Four

"Tee-hee! Tee-hee!" They could hear the queen meach giggling from the meach tree.

"Forget the queen," said Mung. "You're going to have to get past those guards."

Chowder and Shnitzel put their heads together and came up with a plan.

Which is why, five minutes later, they were wearing enormous fake moustaches. Shnitzel was carrying a salesman's case as they approached.

"Greetings," Chowder called to the guards,

holding out a copy of *Meach Monthly* magazine.
"We are selling magazine subscriptions to the
hip, young queen meach on the go. Is your queen
meach at home?"

"Grrrr-aaa!" The guards took one look at them
and attacked!

"It's a very reasonable offer …" added
Chowder before he was hurled into the air.
"Arrrrgh!" he screamed.

"Raaaa!" screamed Shnitzel.

When they landed, Chowder and Shnitzel
tried Disguise Number Two. They returned to
the meach tree wearing white sheets.

"Ra-aa-da," moaned Shnitzel in his best ghost voice.

"Oo-oo-ooh," wailed Chowder.

Surprise, surprise – the guards weren't fooled. **"Grrrr-aaa-aaa!"** they growled as they attacked Chowder and Shnitzel again.

"Arrrrgh!" screamed Chowder as he ran away.

"Raaaa!" screamed Shnitzel, the meach guards **snap-snapping** at his heels with their sharp teeth.

Time for Disguise Number Three.

"Laa-la-la-la-laa," sang Chowder as he and Shnitzel returned wearing Mexican mariachi band outfits with big sombrero hats. Chowder

strummed a guitar while Shnitzel played the trumpet.

"Grrrr-aaa-aaa!" growled the guards as they attacked again.

"Arrrrgh!" screamed Chowder.

"Raaaa!" screamed Shnitzel.

Disguise Number Four was never going to work. Chowder and Shnitzel just didn't look like Girl Guides, even though they were carrying boxes of cookies and talking in little-girl voices.

"Grrrr-aaa-aaa!" growled the guards as they attacked again.

"Arrrrgh!" screamed Chowder.

"Raaaa!" screamed Shnitzel.

Defeated and out of disguises, Chowder and Shnitzel trudged back to the car, where Mung was still hiding. As he was about to tell Mung he was giving up on the meach quest, Chowder had one, last, silly idea.

"Mung, have you ever tried *asking*?" Chowder.

"Hmm ... I never thought of that," he replied. "I was too busy screaming as they chewed my knees to remember my manners."

"Come on, Shnitzel," said Chowder. "I know what must be done."

Walking up to the meach tree, Chowder faced the guards bravely. "Excuse me, we'd like to speak politely for a moment."

"Grrrr! Rrrrr!" The guards just growled and roared in reply, but Chowder was not going to be put off.

"We would be honoured if your queen would return with us to our kitchen," said Chowder nicely. Maybe a little flattery would work on the queen, too. "She is the most delicious fruit in the entire kingdom."

"Tee-hee! Oh, you!" cooed the queen meach, giggling happily.

"And we wish to make her into the most delicious dessert in the whole world," Chowder added.

The queen meach was delighted. "Tee-hee!" she tittered. "Ooo, catch me! Catch me!" and she jumped out of the tree into Shnitzel's arms.

"Ra-ddaa," said a surprised Shnitzel. And he was even more surprised when the queen meach kissed him on the cheek. He blushed as only a rock monster can.

"Wwwwoo-oo-oo!" the guards cheered.

Chowder was amazed. Astonished. Astounded, even. "We did it!" he cried.

"Chowder, being polite worked!" said Mung, equally amazed.

"I know," said Chowder. Then he smiled a sly smile. *"They totally fell for it!"*

Uh-oh.

Chapter Five

Huh? 'Fell for it'? When they heard Chowder's boasts, the meach guards realised that they'd been tricked. They stopped cheering and turned angry again. Very angry. **"Grrrrrrr-oooooo!"** they howled, louder and fiercer than ever!

"Uh, radda," said Shnitzel worriedly.

"Uh-oh," said Chowder. *Oops.*

"Get 'em, boys," ordered the queen meach. She no longer sounded very giggly.

The guards charged. **"Grrrr-aaa-aaa!"**

"No, Chowder," called Mung helpfully as he watched safely from the car. "Don't let 'em rip your arms off. It just makes them angry."

"Arrgh!" screamed Chowder, trying to get his arms back. "Give those back, I need them for cooking!"

"Arrrrgh!"

"Raaaa!"

It was hard for Mung to hear two of his dearest friends crying in such pain. "I can't stand to hear them scream," he muttered to himself, turning up the volume on the car radio to drown them out.

"Arrrrgh! Help, Mung!" cried Chowder.

"La-da-da-da ..." Mung hummed, trying to ignore the terrible sounds as two of the guards clamped Chowder and Shnitzel between their meachy teeth and started to bite and gnaw.

"Shnitzel, if we don't make it out of this, I just want you to know that I used your apron to unclog my toilet," Chowder sobbed between chews.

"Radda-radda?" asked Shnitzel angrily.

"Yeah, it just clogged it up even more," explained Chowder as Shnitzel muttered in fury.

Suddenly, an extra-enormous meach loomed up behind them, its huge jaws stretched wide. **"Grrrrr-oooo!"** it roared, ready to devour its next victim. **"Grrrrr-oooo-oooo!"**

"Arrrrgh!"

"Raaaa!"

Mung couldn't stand by and watch his friends get chomped by an overgrown, overripe meach. He had to do something. "Hold it right there!" he yelled at the meaches.

"Mung?" said Chowder hopefully from the jaws of the meach.

"I want you meaches to know that all your mamas are *dumb* and *ugly*," called Mung bravely.

"Hey, you can't talk dat way 'bout my dumb, ugly mama," growled a meach guard.

"Get 'im, son!" cried the dumbest, ugliest mama meach.

Instantly, the guards attacked!

"Chowder, Shnitzel!" Mung shouted as he ran, the meach guards chasing close behind. "Get the queen meach back to the kitchen. Now! Run! *RUN!*"

Much, much later, Chowder was back in Mung Daal's kitchen, gazing lovingly at his first mince meach pie with the one eye that still worked.

"It's beautiful," he said as the queen meach giggled from inside the pie. "You're my hero, Mung."

"Would you autograph my poster now?" added Chowder, holding up the poster that was now more sticky tape than paper.

"I would be honoured," said Mung from the healing machine where he lay recovering from his injuries.

Mung signed. "There," he said. "Thank you, Chowder, for giving me the courage to foolishly face my entirely rational fears."

"Radda. Radda-radda," said Shnitzel, annoyed. He still had his head, but wore a big bandage where his body had once been, and he was feeling a bit miffed about it.

"Stop complaining," said Mung. "You're getting tomorrow off."

Just then, the mince meach pie customer arrived. "You guys done crying yet?" he snapped.

"Yes, we have," said Mung calmly.

"Here's your pie, Mister," Chowder offered.

"Oo. Well, well," said the customer. He took a deep sniff of the mince meach pie and then ate it in one big mouthful. "I guess this isn't Crybaby Kitchen, after all," he sneered at the damaged trio.

Buuuurp! Uuuuuurp! went the customer rudely. The queen meach laughed happily from inside his stomach. "Tee-hee! I got myself a man," she giggled.

"Well, goodbye," Mung told the pie customer. "And … ah, good luck."

His last words sounded kind of ominous.

"What're you talking about?" the man asked curiously.

Then he got his answer. With a roar, a dozen meach guards appeared out of nowhere and pounced on him.

"Grrrr-aaa-aaa!" snarled the guards.

"Arrrrrgh!" screamed the man. "Arrrrrgh! Oooooo!"

Mung watched smugly as the guards began biting and chewing. "Such a *crybaby*!" he smiled.

THE END